Anonymous

Southern Chivalry

The Adventures of G. Whillikens

Anonymous

Southern Chivalry
The Adventures of G. Whillikens

ISBN/EAN: 9783337294434

Printed in Europe, USA, Canada, Australia, Japan

Cover: Foto ©Raphael Reischuk / pixelio.de

More available books at **www.hansebooks.com**

THE ADVENTURES OF

G. WHILLIKENS, C.S.A.

KNIGHT OF THE GOLDEN CIRCLE;

AND OF

GUINEA PETE,

HIS NEGRO SQUIRE.

AN EPIC·DOGGEREL,
IN SIX BOOKS.

BY A CITIZEN OF THE COTTON COUNTRY.

———◆———

PISTOL.—I know him to be valiant. Faith! he told me so with his own mouth.—*Shakespeare.*

———◆———

CONTENTS.

SOUTHERN CHIVALRY.

BOOK I.

THE NULLIFIER.

Invocation—The Subject hinted—The Principal Character trotted out—He steals Molasses—Old Man Whillikens—Our Hero's Education—He smells Mice—The Nullifier—Secession—Coercion — Old Hickory—Guinea Pete—The Picture of G. Whillikens—Fashion for the Ladies—How the Knight was Mounted—Picture of Guinea Pete—Chat between G. Whillikens and John C. Calhoun—The God of War Invoked—Old Hickory to be cleaned out—Mars discharged and Jupiter engaged—Signs in the Sky—A Council of War—Suggestion of Peter—The Great Nullifier's Prophecy—Orders to "March!" and a general Stampede.

MUSES, like nine sweet nightingales,
Sing the good song of cotton bales;
Of glorious Southern Chivalry;
Of freedom based on slavery;
Of patriarchal negrodom;
Of fiddlesticks, and fife and drum;
Of Southern rights, bombast and bluster,
And of the famous fillibuster,
My hero! From your lofty skies,
Look on me with your eighteen eyes,
And tune my banjo while I sit
And strike, that I may make a hit.

My humble prayer is that I may
Concoct a poem that shall pay
The reader for the reading.   Be
Propitious, pretty Nine, to me,
And you shall see the truth stick out,
Straight as an elephantine snout.

My poem's epic-doggerel,
   (If that is not a gross misnomer ;)
And I have stirring things to tell,
   Of heroes brave as those of Homer.

I sing, lest in the future ages
The worthies of the present stages
   Should be forgotten—lost in fog :
I trot out demigods and sages,
And give to every one his wages :
   I wouldn't hurt a dog.

But I have one especial hero,
Brave as Blue-beard, good as Nero,
'Round whom my other worthy wights
Revolve as naught but satellites.
This hero is G. Whillikens !
Oh, had I Phœnix quills for pens,
I never could write down the fame
That clusters, dustlike, 'round his name :—
How, with the feather of a goose,
Can I his glory reproduce ?
Alas ! 'tis vain.   In simple verse
His worthy exploits I rehearse,
Leaving each deed to preach away
Its hero's merits as it may.

I'll tell you first of little George,
Stealing molasses.   He did gorge
His little abdomen.   His daddy
Detected him.   The old man had a
Hard face.   He cried, with frowning brow,
"You're into the molasses now !"

" No, sir," quoth George, for don't you see,
Th' molasses is all into me ?"

When little Georgy Washington
Hacked a fine cherry tree for fun ;
And, (when his father tracked him to it,)
Owned it, but didn't go to do it,
The old man, pleased to find a youth
But six years old who told the truth,
Laid down his whip and loudly cried,
" Come—I'm amazed !—you haven't lied !
Come to my arms—sit on my knee,
I'm glad you cut the cherry-tree !"

Old Whillikens knew what to do:
He threshed his Georgy black and blue.

This is the only anecdote
The careful reader has to note,
Of our great champion's early life—
His chapter first in scenes of strife.
I set it down that you may see
The dawn of his great destiny.

Old Whillikens had had full swing
Cobbling old shoes, and doctoring
Fiddles and broken china.　But,
Tired of his own Connecticut,
Tired of his trade, down in the mouth,
He sought his fortune in the South ;
Became at first an overseer ;
Laid by his wages year by year ;
Bought a plantation, and began
To be a " Rural Gentleman."

When Whillikens became a planter,
He changed his character *instanter*,
So that our George could curse and swear,
And whoop and halloo every where ;
Could crack the negroes o'er the head,

And kick his brothers out of bed;
Could chew tobacco, spit and smoke,
While not a word the old man spoke.
At school, a dozen boys together
Thought it fine fun to tar and feather
The poor schoolmaster. In this sport
George was the leader, if report
Does not belie him. His old sire
First told his son he was a liar;—
Then, when an oath confirmed its truth,
Laughed loudly at the hopeful youth;
Laughed loudly at the teacher's plight,
And gave the verdict "Sarved him right."

Thus, bless'd with good association,
Our hero got his education;
Performed a thousand clever tricks,
With wealthy, spirited young bricks;
And not a mutter of reproof
Was heard 'neath the paternal roof.
I do believe, with such young asses,
He might have stolen dad's molasses.

Trot on, trot on, ye lazy muses,
Before the reader's eye refuses
To follow in so slow a pace;
Spur up, and bring us to the place
In this historiography
Where heroes show their chivalry—
At least, where our most hopeful wight
Shall wear the belt and badge of knight.

Well! George had sported a goat-tee,
And worn his pistols and bowie,
Played euchre and drank whiskey toddy,
'Till he was big as any body.

Now, when he'd met a clever fellow,
And exchanged powder in duello;
Had shot a squirrel, tarred a teacher,

And helped to hang a traveling preacher,
He sighed to find a wider field,
Where genius could be more revealed :
He prayed the stars to grant him luck
And give him chance to show his pluck.

As he stirred up ambition's coals,
And snuffed the smoke in his nose-holes ;
As he was just about to sneeze,
There came upon the passing breeze
A strong gunpowder stink.   He rose
And lifted higher up his nose :—
The scent had come from Caroliny,
(Not from the land of forests piney,
For there was not a sniff of tar,)
It surely had the smell of war ;
It came from the Palmetto Tree,
The land of rice and chivalry,
Chock-full of Jews.

   Now, mount up higher,
My flock of muses.   I aspire
To sing the noble nullifier—
The man who wrote through days and nights
To prove " The South should have her rights ;"
But didn't think he could " secede"
Unless he had some wrong to plead ;
Didn't think a State could bolt
From the enclosure, like a colt,
Unless some " compact" first be broken—
And this great sage was not a jokin'.
Well, that denies, beyond a doubt,
That States may, *at their will*, go out ;
Denies that any one may fly,
And scorn to tell the reason why :
So I suspect this worthy leader
Was, after all, a poor seceder.
But when you come to nullifying,
You see his streamers all a-flying.
He thought within the federation,

His State could rule the Yankee nation;
Could give the only true solution
To questions on the Constitution;
Could disregard judicial powers,
And over-ride this land of ours
Just like a nightmare.   He would creep
Out of his way to kick a sheep;
And now, with all his might and will,
Had kicked up at a tariff bill,
And put his foot in't.   Hence arose
The great war-stench; for there were those
To take up arms to prove by fight,
Ad hominem, that he was right—
Right in the quarts of ink he shed,
To make folks follow where he led;
Right all about the Constitution,
Tariff, sheep and dissolution.

South Carolinians, who shall dare
To raise the hand to touch a hair
Of your sweet persons?   Who oppose
Such blooded and chivalric foes?
'Twould be "coercion."   You should do
Whatever Calhoun tells you to,
And let the nation stand aghast,
And bend the head before the blast.
Come war, come death, come even worse—
The Government must not "coerce,"
But stand a quiet, peaceful ghost,
While Carolina rules the roast.

Alas! alas! alas! alas!
What shameful thing did come to pass!·
Old Hickory was president:
And straight to work the old fool went,
Proclaiming what he meant to do,
Id est, flog all the valiant crew—
Yea, flog South Carolina's sons,
Her "gentlemen" and her big guns,
Till, like spanked babies they should cry,
And promise not to nullify.

Thus was the land on war's dread brink,
When brave G. Whillikens smelt the stink.
He swore, he snorted, raised his bristles,
Flourshed his bowie, snapt his pistols ;
And while his ardor was most fervent,
Summoned his faithful body servant,
(A roguish, grinning, saucy cheat,
Called by the negroes, " Guinea Pete,")
And swore in good round oaths to Peter
He'd live and die a true fire-eater.
" Hope massa will not burn his mouth,"
Said the sly native of the South.
Then said the master to his man,
" Get ready, Pete, quick as you can—
Quick, you black rascal, sleek and shiny,
I'm going off to Caroliny ;
I feel my bosom growing larger,
Go and bring out my fine gray charger !"
Quoth Pete, " Oh, massa, I'm a fool
If dat gray charger aint a mule."
" Hush, blockhead ! do not move so slow,
I mean that you shall also go."
" Yes, Sir," said Pete, whose wit grew duller,
" Dat is a hoss of nuther color."

My poem would fall short by half,
Without my hero's photograph ;
So here, before he goes to battle
To fight the loyal hireling cattle,
I'll stop and take it, or I'll try :
G. Whillikens was five feet high
And three feet through or figures lie ;
Thick-necked, broad-shouldered, double fisted,
With big bowlegs a little twisted ;
A nose like Bardolph's, large and red,
A hairy face, a bushy head
All full of phrenologic bumps,
(Created by successive thumps),
And bulging out with brains behind,
Because he carried there his mind ;

Besides, he had, like men of yore,
Head over heels and breast before.

G. Whillikens had two gray eyes,
Popped forward, of tremendous size :
Hence is this child of chivalry
Styled, " Gray-eyed man of destiny."

This picture may be overdrawn
   About the nose and waist and shoulder,
But it will serve as we go on,
   And be complete when he grows older.

Perhaps the ladies, ere he goes,
Would hear about my hero's clothes.
'Twas my design to state before
That our brave salamander wore
Costume of Georgia volunteers—
Shirt collar and a pair of spurs,
With clothes between.   A bloody strip
Ran up each shank from heel to hip ;
His bobtailed coat of rusty gray,
With big bell buttons bright and gay,
And epaulettes of golden brass
Would take the eye of any lass.
A belt was round his waist extended
From which his " tooth-pick" was suspended ;
A sword was also buckled to it,
Which dragged the ground where'er he drew it.
A big chapeau, with one bright star
Screwed on in front, and seen afar,
Made up our hero's uniform
When going forth to breast the storm
Of that dread war.

          How he was mounted
I do not think need be recounted ;
Whether he sat upon his ass,
Or horse, like good Sir Hudibras ;
Whether he rode a rawboned shanty,

Such as Don Quixote's Rosinante ;
Whether he rode, like Yankee Doodle,
Upon a poney (*a horse-poodle ;*)
Whether on Bucephalian steed,
One of Great Alexander's breed ;
Whether, like Porus, off he went
Upon an awful elephant ;
Or like Judge T——, in gown and wig
Went on a-creaking in a gig ;
Or like some knightly Esquimaux,
Rode, driving dog-team through the snow ;
Or, like Siberian Betsey, put
Best leg before and went afoot ;
Or like Dave Crockett, hunting boars,
Rode through the briars on all fours,
'Tis useless further to detail.
He mostly rode upon a rail
Propelled by steam.

     'Tis not my style
To stop and draw a slave's profile,
I'll merely say that Squire Guinea,
(Born and brought up in " old Virginny,"
And sold down South for running away,
Also, for money,) was a gay
And sprightly darkey, with sharp features,
More so than most of colored creatures.
He was, (to draw him at one dash,)
Worth eighteen hundred dollars cash.
Dressed out in bagging *cap-a-pie,*
He holds the chargers, gray and bay—
A mule and jackass, meant to go
No farther than the first *depot.*

Steam and chain-lightning ! what a bound !
Pegasus has leaped o'er the ground,
Our knight so fat, and squire so shiny
Are in " Chivalrous Caroliny,"
Holding a chat with that old coon,
The patriot sage, John C. Calhoun.

The latter talked of Southern rights,
And said he couldn't sleep o' nights
Because the tariff did not sit
Well on his stomach.   He had writ
Books, speeches, and wise cogitations
Upon the rights of sov'reign nations;
Had demonstrated slavery,
The corner stone of liberty;
But still the people would not think !˙
It hurt his stomach.   "Take a drink ?"
Said brave G. Whillikens; and Pete
Pulled out his flask and gave a treat.
" Now let us talk about the war,"
Said Whillikens.   " I wear the star
That rises to proclaim the hour
Of freedom wrung from fed'ral power.
I come to lead your gallant band,
Victorious o'er Columbia's land;
To whip Old Hickory to terms,
˙And give his carcass to the worms—
Hip, hip, hurrah !"

                    Great rabble groups
Of " patriarchs" stood 'round for troops.
" South Carolinians, who shall be
The chief to lead to victory ?
Fire-eaters, who's the salamander
Worthy to be your own commander ?"
Thus shouted the great Nullifier,
When voices high, and voices higher
Exclaimed, with many loud " amens !"
" G. Whillikens ! G. Whillikens !!"

O thou, the god of bloody wars,
   With Flight and Terror for thy steeds,
Thou great fire-eating, mighty Mars,
   Teach me to sing of noble deeds !

Now, o'er the rice-fields, hear the hum
Of moving mass and growling drum—

The Chivalry ! they come ! they come !
They come to whip the government.
The very air is redolent
With streaks of whiskey fume and gas
Where'er the valiant Quixotes pass ;
The very dust is painted ruddy,
Stirred up by " patriarchs" so bloody ;
The very sky is blue with curses,
(With which I'll not adorn my verses ;)
The very sunbeams from their steel
Rebound.   They come with tramping heel,
Led onward by the great fire-eater,
And his man Friday, Guinea Peter.

Old Hick'ry, what are you to do ?
You must not bring your hireling crew
Against such well-bred gentlemen.
You can't expect a citizen,
At your request, sir, to enlist
And be a vile "submissionist,"
Bad as an " abolitionist ?"
You can't expect a patriot
With your vile cause to cast his lot
And help you to defeat our plot ?
You cannot think the constitution
Supports you in your resolution
To keep it sacred from pollution ?
Old man, you put yourself in clover
By fighting when the war was over,
When, long ago, at New Orleans
You whipt the British " just for greens ;"
But never yet—oh, never yet
Such men as these are, have you met :
Therefore, prepare to take a drumming—
The *patriarchal boys* are coming !

Mars, I requested thee to teach
  Me how to sing of war : I wonder
Whether I must again beseech
  Thee to put in a little thunder !

Surely the Muses can't knock under
   And sing a war without a battle?
Surely 'twould be a mighty blunder—
   A war-song where no bullets rattle!
Mars, I discharge thee. Jupiter,
   Come forward with your thunderbolt,
And give the sacred Nine a stir,
   As with a sharp stick; make 'em jolt
On Pegasus—or on the colt,
   Which may get on a little faster;
So, let them leave the jaded dolt
   To browse at pleasure in the pasture,
While all the Nine shall sit astraddle,
And ride the young nag without saddle
O Jupiter, grant this I pray,
And put some thunder in my lay.

G. Whillikens was death on rats,
And death on union democrats,
And death upon the president,
And death upon the government,
"All in a horn." He bravely fought
Great battles, and great triumphs wrought
In glorious Dreamland. His brave boys,
With Pete, fife, drum, and other noise,
Could make the country all their own,
If they were "only let alone."

While blood was in newspapers streaming,
And thunders roaring, lightnings gleaming,
Armies marching, soldiers swearing,
Suddenly there was a staring!
Signs were in the firmament,
Showing that the president
Had the people at his back,
Ready all to toe the track;
Ready all, with sword and gun
To battle for the Union.
"THE UNION!" they cried, unswerved,
"It *must be*—it SHALL BE preserved!"

These unexpected signs confounded
The patriarchal boys.   They'd grounded
Their calculations on the hope
That Hick'ry would not use the rope
To baste their backs ; nor as a halter
To stretch their necks.   The gents did falter,
And hold war council.   Guinea Pete
Said " Massa never will retreat
Before the poor, white Northern trash."
(The sly black fox deserved the lash,
For I believe the selfish larkie
Thought such a war would free the darkey.)
Up jumped a gent when Pete said that,
Exclaiming, " Boys, I smell a rat :
I'm going home to my plantation
To let alone the slave relation."
A dozen officers or more
Said they were going too, but swore
They did not fear Old Hick'ry's arm—
They felt no symptoms of alarm ;
But, while the mad old fool was plotting,
They thought they'd *better be a-trotting.*

Now rose the sage, John C. Calhoun,
Pale as the man up in the moon,
And, with a seer's prophetic tongue,
The present and the future sung.
Thus said the great philosopher :
" Car'lina is ' mine oyster.'
She'll leave the Union at the hour
When Northern votes shall have the power
To govern by majority :
(A *democrat* I claim to be.)
Now, if we work our cards aright,
When she goes out, sirs, just for spite,
The other slave states, altogether,
Like sheep behind some big bell-wether,
Will jump the fence and follow after."
This speech produced a little laughter ;
And then the prophet said his State
   2

Was chivalrous and very great ;
" But friends," said he, " your present pallor
Betrays the better part of valor.
Brave as a Turk, fierce as a Hessian,
You've something more than pluck, *discretion.*
We'll have to back out now, my men,
To bide our time 'to hit again ;'
We'll have to get the South united,
Pretending to have wrong things righted ;
We'll have to lay a deeper plot,
And strike—not till the iron's hot."

This speech created such a bluster,
It waked our embryo fillibuster,
Who rolled his eyes, and felt his spunk,
And loudly swore he wasn't drunk ;
Rose to his feet and wabbled 'round
With broadsword trailing on the ground ;
Cried " Forward march !" so very clever,
All yelled " G. Whillikens forever !"

Our hero had been drunk and dozing
While sages were their plans disclosing ;
Had been of glorious battles dreaming,
While gentlemen their flight were scheming ;
And, knowing nothing said or done,
Had meant to march on Washington :
Thanks to his grog !

                    Did troops obey ?
They marched—*but marched the other way.*

Thus Carolinians in revolt,
  When Jupiter had made a blunder,
And lent the foe his thunderbolt,
  Took to their heels to bolt the thunder !

BOOK II.

THE FIRE-EATER.

Southern Wrongs to be Righted—Southern " Commercial"
 Convention—The Order of the Golden Circle Organized—
 The First Degree—Tariff—Commerce—The Souls of Slaves
 —Negro Negro-drivers—Choctaw Negro-drivers—South-
 ern Literature—Non-intercourse with the North—Tickling
 the Funny-bone—"Nigger," "Nigger," "Nigger"—G.
 Whillikens dubbed Knight—Peter dubbed Squire—Their
 Mission—Red-headed Critics Rebuked—Our Knight as a
 Logician—He is Assisted by New-comers in the South
 —Our Hero's fat Fist gets bruised—The Squire takes it
 into his head to take to his heels—Caught by Blood-
 hounds—Runs away again with his Master's Consent—
 Helps to increase the Public Agitation.

Now flap your wings, my flock of Muses,
    And bear me onward in my flight ;
If any one of you refuses,
    I'll dock her tail this very night.

Twenty years of meditation
Whillikens, on his plantation,
Pass'd with Peter.   Hark ! he hears,
Within his two uncotton'd ears,
News that the Southern chivalry
Are waking from their lethargy.
"Pete," said our hero, "catch my mare—
My country calls ! I'll do my share
By strength of arm, or word of mouth,
To right the wrongs of my dear South."

How Peter put the bridle on,
Be silent, Muse !   Our knight had gone

(19)

But three days with his trusty Pete,
Before his journey was complete.
Then he beheld the South a-swelling,
To get up something worth the telling.

The upshot of the mighty toil
   Was a "commercial" convocation,
Where " patriarchs" of Southern soil
   Consulted for the Southern nation.
The upshot of the consultation
   Among the stirring chivalry
Was a bran-new organization,
   The Golden Circle, First Degree.

The Order boasted three degrees ;
   It had its wheels within its wheels ;
It had its cross-bones, swords and keys ;
   It had its secret signs and seals.
Woe to the brother who reveals
   The secrets of the sacred order,
Imparted to him, while he kneels
   And curses all beyond its border !
His broad-cloth coat and patent leathers,
Would be exchanged for tar and feathers.

The outer wheel, or first degree,
Proposed to meet " commercially,"
Though it was but a talking meeting.
The members gave each other greeting ;
Preached piously about their "duties,"
Silks, calicoes and other beauties ;
All simple " customs" they decried,
While Cotton King was deified.
One said, " Free trade, free ships, free state"—
   " Abusing freedom of debate,
And out of order," said the chair.
" It slipped out ere I was aware,"
Explained the member, fighting Kitty,
Who hailed from the Palmetto city.
A Texan said, " We must prepare
A Southern commerce."   Then and there,

The members, showing that they knew it,
Raised a committee *just to do it.*
A preacher, just to show his wit,
Proved negroes slaves by holy writ ;
Proved slavery is good—in fine
The institution is divine.
A doctor, an anatomist,
Spoke of the negro's horny fist,
His gizzard foot, his sable skin,
And his peculiar make within,
And wisely said, upon the whole
He thought the negro had no soul.
Uprose a colored gentleman,
Black as a stove or frying pan,
With nose ungristled, woolly head,
And with red, mushy lips, he said,
" I'm a slaveholder ; I have thirty,
All of them ignorant and dirty.
I hold the negroes, don't you see,
In *my superiority.*
Denounce my race, not as a whole,
But merely say *slaves* have no soul,
And I will advocate, you see,
The doctor's new psychology."
A gentleman from Arkansas,
Attorney—Counselor-at-law,
New England Poet—Indian Chief,
Rose, promising to be most brief,
But perpetrated, then and there,
A speech as lengthy as his hair,
Which came so far below his jaw,
Some thought the Chief an Indian squaw.
He said th' enlightened Choctaw Nation,
Well understood the slave relation,
Leaving his native home " down East,"
Behind the age, a league at least ;
That red-skin negro-drivers made
The best of masters, and would aid
The Southern cause in any strife,
With tomahawk and scalping knife.

An editor from Cincinnati,
(Now of the Orleans literati,)
Whom some call "Judge," contrived to "rile"
The Chief, by comments on his style.
This served the conference to vary,
And make it somewhat literary.
A Vicksburg minister was sure
The South should have "A Literature,"
And Southern books for Southern schools,
Lest children learn by Northern rules.
A sly Mercurial editor,
A Carolina man-o'-war,
With knowing wink, said, "Paper-readers
Should not read aught but Southern leaders;
And if you are true blue," he hinted,
"Find where your magazines are printed."
　　Professor J. D. B. De B.,
Was on his pegs right speedily,
And from his tall, two-story head,
Let out an idea, and said,
That though he printed in the North,
His readers had their money's worth.
Then spoke the crooked statistician
At length, defining his position;
Making a rigmarole discourse,
To advocate "non-intercourse"
With Northern people, who were all
An abolitionized cabal.
　　Then rose a dozen gents, or more—
Each loudly claimed to have the floor;
And, as the chair cared not a feather,
It let them jabber altogether.
They chattered lovingly as brothers,
Just to tickle one another's
Funny bone.　And then they lifted
Up their voices, rarely gifted,
Just to talk of Southern glory.
Then into the second story
Of their eloquence, they clamber'd;
And the air was badly hammer'd

By their claws ; while not a single
Word of all they did commingle,
Came to little, big or bigger,
But the sound of " nigger," " nigger,"
 " Nigger," " nigger" everywhere,
Till the sound of " nigger," " nigger,"
Made our Guinea Peter snigger,
 " White folks is oncommon queer."

I will not stop to quote debates,
Since all such stuff the reader hates,
And since I've given all the sense
Of much first-rate grandiloquence.
I can't repeat all that was done ;
 Perhaps 'tis only necessary
To say the Circle quit their fun,
 To dub our hero " Missionary"—
An " Errant-knight" to ride about
 And "set the Southern heart on fire ;"
And Guinea Pete, there is no doubt,
 Was formally ordained a squire.

When the dubbing rites were over,
Whillikens became a rover,
O'er the cotton-country trotting,
Talking, cursing, boasting, plotting,
Southern injuries proclaiming,
Southern independence naming,
Northern progress deprecating,
Northern march of mind debating,
Wouldn't hush.   It was his mission
To direct the politician ;
Teach the noisy demagogue,
Better how to play the dog ;
Teach the editors of papers,
Better how to " cut their capers ;"
Teach them all to stir the coals
Of strife and hate in Southern souls,
Till, cursing institutions free,
They should e'en boast of slavery,
" The corner stone of liberty."

Red-headed critics may suppose
  That Whillikens and Pete the squire,
Could not control such men as those,
  And set the Southern heart on fire.
To such I'd say, My learned lark,
You've very widely missed the mark.
Did not our hero wear a dirk,
And swear to fighting like a Turk?
Drank he not whiskey? Did he not
Condemn the North to regions hot?
Could he not bluster, swell and sweat,
And back his logic by a bet?
Was he not great at argument
On slavery, where'er he went,
Convincing all, or hushing them
By argument *ad hominem?*
Could he not shake his mighty fist,
And cry "You're abolitionist!"
And would that whip-cord not suffice,
To make opponents still as mice?
As to the squire, he served first rate,
The arguments to illustrate;
All which I may hereafter show,
And I may not—can't tell, you know.

G. Whillikens was much assisted
By those who had but late enlisted
In the good cause. Men of the North,
Who to the South had journeyed forth,
Out-hectored Hector in the rattle
They made in chaining human cattle.
All Southern editors, I know,
Were yankee babies, long ago;
Three-fourths of Southern officers
Were yankee boys in other years;
One half the negro-traders, too,
Were yankee youths with bellies blue;
And many red-mouthed Southern speakers,
Were what they now call "freedom shriekers."
But south of Mason-Dixon's line,
Of yankee sins they loudly whine,

Lest they, perchance, should be suspected,
Or have their early creed detected.

With such good help, you well may guess,
G. Whillikens had much success,
As he, for twenty months or more,
Preached " Southern rights" from shore to shore,
Leading his converts where he chose,
With secret man-hooks in the nose.

Said Peter, " Wonder if de whites
Aint workin' for de niggers' rights !"
There may have been a meaning in it,
But Whillikens did not unskin it.
" A nigger has no rights," he said,
Knocking his comrade on the head ;
" You woolly ' abolitionist,'
If you again bruise up my fist,
I'll whip you till you do confess,
And then I'll hang you for redress."
Pete answered with humility,
" Masser has been too good to me ;
A hundred licks is my desert,
I's sorry Masser's fist is hurt."
G. Whillikens was more composed,
And said, " I'll not repeat my blows ;
But as to ' rights,' don't make pretense :
Niggers are fools—they've got no sense."
" That's so," said Peter, as he coughed,
" We niggers' heads is mighty soft."

Thus Whillikens did illustrate
The negro's blest contented state ;
Thus did he seem to prove, at least,
The negro nothing but a beast.

Said Peter to himself one day,
" I'll just cut stick and run away ;"
And off he scamper'd o'er the grounds,
Till overtaken by the hounds.

G. Whillikens, with twenty more
In hot pursuit, came up before
The " nigger-dogs" had made their dinner
Upon the beastly chattel-sinner.
The master kind cursed Pete two hours,
And then, with patriarchal powers,
Brought out the cowhide, when the squire
Cried to the knight, " I did desire
To help de boss to agitate ;
I jist did go to illustrate
De mighty wrongs ob abolition,
And, as yer squire, to fill my mission."

" Good !" cried the vain, outwitted master,
" Do it again, and scamper faster ;
I know no nigger yet has gotten
Out of the empire of King Cotton,
But I will take you to Kentucky
Where runaways have been more lucky ;
Then to Ohio you will travel—
I'll advertise and play the devil ;
I'll get, besides my property,
Free niggers for indemnity.
Thus we'll get up a great sensation,
Throughout this philanthropic nation."

This strange *programme*, there's no doubt,
Was to the letter carried out,
But here, alas ! the Muses fail
To give the exploit in detail.

Thus did the squire perform his part,
In firing up the Southern heart ;
Riding all day for Southern rights,
And fiddling for his boss o'nights.

Now, Muses, you may go to roost,
    Upon Parnassus, or a tree ;
The big spread eagle shall be loosed
    To flap me through the next degree

BOOK III.

THE FILLIBUSTER.

The Golden Circle, Second Degree—Speech of G. Whillikens
—Old John of York—Speech of a little Jew—March of
Civilization to be opposed—The "Area of Freedom" to be
extended—Side remark by Guinea Pete—Speech of
another Peter—Aaron Burr lived too early—Expedition
to Cuba—Gathering of the Clans—Lopez—The Captain-
general of Cuba, and his hosts, badly frightened—Lopez
caught in the chaparral by "nigger-dogs"—G. Whillikens caught "taking water," and confined in Moro Castle
—Pete's opinion of the Expedition—Raid upon Nicaragua
—Billy Walker and G. Whillikens—Adventures in Honduras—The Southernizing of Kansas—The Golden Circle
fails to spread itself.

WHEN the Circle, first degree,
Had executed its decree,
And Whillikens had done his part
In "firing up the Southern heart,"
The members were together beckoned,
For session in degree the second.
The doors were brought-to with a crash—
Without were left the "poor white trash;"
Within were our G. Whillikens
And the most worthy citizens.

When all had shown by signs and grips,
By putting elbows on the hips,
By certain squints and certain thumps,
That all within the hall were "trumps,"
The great G. Whillikens arose,
With his Bardolphian big nose,
With his Falstaffian dimensions,
Becoming well his slight pretensions,

(27)

And thus most modestly began :
" My boys, I am the ' Gray-eyed Man
Of Destiny.'   I called this meeting
For something more than friendly greeting.
I've stirred the people up like mush ;
And now I want to make a rush,
And whip somebody.   I'm your man,
If you'll devise some fighting plan.
You say the South is out of joint.
Now, come up to the sticking point ;
Give me a regiment or more,
And I can march from shore to shore,
And with my knighthood's flag unfurled,
Whip all the cowards in the world,—
Hip, hip, hurrah !"

            A fine old man
Sat meditating on some plan.
'Twas good old John, (once of New York,)
With face as red as pickled pork,
The Earl of Houma, the blest saint
Who meekly bears without complaint
Grave charges of election frauds,
And merely mutters, " Darn the odds."
Behind him stood a lad of promise,
Born on the island of St. Thomas,
A very pretty little Jew,
Who did whate'er John told him to.
His name was Judas—he had not
The surname of Iscariot.
At good old John's command, he said,
" Let's bring our counsels to a head ;
The sunny South, in evil hour,
Has lost the prestige of her power ;
She can no longer rule the roast,
By fiery threat and idle boast.
The yankees count so many noses,
They're bound to rule, whoe'er opposes ;
They have *more women than have we*,
And thus they'll make the new states free.

All nature seems to help them on ;
We must *do* something, or we're gone !
The North is growing greater, greater,
And it must sooner, sirs, or later,
By numbers rule. We must assuage
The onward progress of the age,
Or reinstate our former powers
By adding other lands to ours."
    Here there was deafening applause,
With thumping heels and clapping claws.
    He further said the Southrons should
Extend their borders if they could ;
Said that the star of empire squinted
A little southerly, and hinted
Of new states cut from Mexico,
Where slavery was sure to go ;
Of rich West India plantations
Stocked full of slaves, the wealth of nations ;
Of Cuba, yearning now to be
Joined to our land of liberty.

A hundred yells of loud applause
Approved this speech in Cuba's cause ;
A hundred men swore lustily,
" Down-trodden Cuba shall be free !
The South shall have her fortunes mended
By having Freedom's bounds extended,
And our ' peculiar institution'
Shall be the Union's dissolution,
Or rule the roast, as it has done
E'er since the days of Washington."
    " Just so," said Pete, (somewhat in liquor),
" You spread the thing to make it thicker."

Said Whillikens unto the Jew,
" Sweet Judas, what d'ye mean to *do ?*"
"'Take Cuba, knight ; at least we'll try it,
And master John says we can buy it ;
With thirty millions, 'tis quite plain,
We'll buy it from the queen of Spain."

Up rose a brown-faced chevalier,
Whose soul had never known a fear—
'Twas Houma's well beloved friend,
Chivalrous Peter of Ostend,
" Amer'can senator" from France.
No prouder knight e'er bore a lance ;
For when away in Spain on furlough,
He fought and vanquished Monsieur Turgot.
    He rolled his eyes and looked around,
Prepared to utter truths profound,
And clenched his fist up, just to shake it ;
"If we want Cuba, *we must take it !*
We've got the man, this big game rooster,
G. Whillikens, the filibooster ;
And I predict, from his char-ac-ter,
He'll prove a creole benefactor.
We've got Narcisco Lopez, he
Who longs to set white Cubans free ;
The man who bravely fought in war
'Gainst liberty and Bolivar.
We've got our Quitman, (born up north),
Johnston and Thrasher, and so forth,
And Henningsen and Guinea Pete,
And many more 'as good as *Wheat.*'
With such warm Southern bloods as these,
We'll whip the queen of Antilles !
    "If 'tis the purpose of the Order,
We may extend our southern border
And take poor Nicaragua in,
For long ago it should have been
A land of slaves and liberty.
We've got the man just fit to be
Poor Nicaragua's Alexander
The Great.   This embryo commander
Has a most awful hankering
After the proud Mosquito king ;
He has a taste, (he does assure us,)
For making conquests in Honduras ;
He'll see Central America
Enclosed in ' Freedom's area.'

This hero is the silent talker,
The mighty little Billy Walker.
Of course he'll not go forth to fight
But with our Golden Circle knight.
Thus, gentlemen, the South shall shine
With many stars.   The cause divine
Shall triumph over 'abolition,'
And Whillikens perform his mission."

" Huzza! huzza !" the Circle cried,
And thumping heels were multiplied ;
Such speeches made the brotherhood
Stroke up their whiskers and feel good.
Said Guinea Pete, sly as an eel,
" De white folks say de niggers steal."

Scream out your grand whangdoodle now,
    Spread-eagle bird !   The hills and glens
All echo with a loud pow-wow,
    " G. Whillikens !" " G. Whillikens ! !"

Let no law-loving puritan
Stick up his nose at this good man.
Let no one think he was a robber
Because he was a fighting-jobber.
Who shines with more resplendent lustre
Than Aaron Burr, the fillibuster ?
Who ever got in water hotter
For being nothing but a plotter ?
Alas ! he lived one generation
Too early for this fast young nation !
Old fogies could not estimate
The value of this man of state.
Shame on my country !   Must my verse
Say that the nation did " coerce"
This gent, who merely meant to go
And take the South to Mexico ?

Shade of great Captain Kidd, draw near,
And o'er my country drop a tear ;

Wipe out this blot upon her page,
And write that Burr surpassed his age.

Now Guinea Peter and his master
Are going fast and going faster
Upon their very holy mission,
The modern gold-fleece expedition
To conquer Cuba.   The extension
Of Freedom's area they mention,
As the praiseworthy enterprise
Before our hero's two gray eyes.

G. Whillikens had blown his trumpet,
    Something like old Roderick Dhu,
And a crowd of noble loafers
    Had come on to make his crew.
Some had come from brave Kentucky,
    From " Virginia's sacred soil,"
Some from braggart Mississippi,
    Some from hard state-prison toil,
Some from elsewhere—all to battle ;
All to hear the bullets rattle ;
All to smoke, and drink, and muster,
With our gray-eyed fillibuster.
"How kind," said Pete, " de poor white trash **are**,
To serve rich folks and Mr. Thrasher !"

Ho ! for the islands of the sea !
The Pompero bears liberty !
The " area of freedom" stretches
To circumscribe the Cuban wretches.

As some big hen-hawk dashes down
    Upon a flock of frightened chickens,
So came G. Whillikens' frown,
    Scaring the Cubans " like the dickens."

Behind that frown the hero came—
    Narcisco Lopez on his right ;

The Spanish soldiers heard the name,
    And grasped their rifles in affright!

Ah! so affrighted were they all
    About the sugar lands and niggers,
That loading up with minie ball,
    They, in their panic, pulled the triggers!

The triggers caused the balls to fly—
    The flying caused the freedom spreaders
To spread themselves, and not to try
    Their arms, before they tried their treaders!

Some with old Lopez broke and ran
    Into the shady chaparral,
Where each good blood-hound found his man,
    And grabbed his breeches, *just to smell.*

Some with G. Whillikens and Pete,
    His ever faithful negro vassal,
Were paddling water in retreat
    When caught and put in Moro Castle.

And there they lay, bereft of rum,
Hearing each morn the rolling drum;
Not knowing whether 'twas their lot
To be *garroted*, or be shot,
Until the Spanish captain did
Consign them home *via* Madrid.
    "Pete," said the hero of the mission,
"What think you of the expedition?"
With countenance of mischief full,
Quoth Pete, "All cry and little wool."

Imagination, with thy painted wings,
Fly in the readers' brains. The poet sings
Not of the triumphs of the chivalry,
When Billy Walker made savannahs free
In Nicaragua; when his naval fleet
Was with one oyster-boat esteemed complete,
  3

While his brave army had their choicest pickins
In taking off the saucy Costa Ricans ;
When Billy, as historians assure us,
Made fillibuster marches on Honduras,
And made a fame, and did so much to swell it
I cannot take the trouble here to tell it.
All this, Imagination, I shall leave,
For you to pencil.   Fail not to conceive
That great G. Whillikens was at the bottom
Of Billy's works.   I'm sorry I've forgot 'em.

Well, when these raids so sweetly planned ;
     With such benevolent intention ;
So sagely laid, so bravely manned,
     Had given Southrons no *extension ;*
And when they were about to *fail,*
     Like gentlemanly bankrupt dandies,
G. Whillikens had hit the nail,
     And gone up North to fight on Kansas.
He battled there with desperation,
To widen out the Southern Nation ;
Down went 'Missouri compromise'—
Down went the South up to the eyes,
And Whillikens in his own gutter,
Wabbled, and made so great a splutter
That Guinea Peter did not fail
To pull him out by his coat-tail ;
And, as he leisurely did pull it,
Remarked, "De ballot and de bullet
Are both agin ye, masser."

                         What
Resulted from the Kansas Plot ?
The Southern area remained
Within its own confines enchained ;
It would not spread itself like blubber,
It would not stretch like Indian rubber.

Said Guinea Pete, " We've had bad luck ;
De 'Institution' has got stuck ;

But oh ! it was de best of fancies,
To take de cotton hands to Kansas."

G. Whillikens had done his best,
And added laurels to his crest ;
Resolved, he gave the marching word,
And went to seek Degree the Third.

BOOK IV.

THE CONSPIRATOR.

G. Whillikens and Guinea before the Grotto of the Third
Degree—No Quorum—Uses of this Inner Wheel—Peep—
An Inner Wheel within this Inner Wheel—Two Loving
Friends in Council—The Superhuman and the Inhuman
—Treason in Spirit and in Act—Its relation to Hemp—
Contract between the Devil and somebody else—Calhoun's Prophecy—The South to be bedeviled and made
to "go it Blind"—Hornet's Nests to be avoided—One of
the Sweet Williams—Two Duelling Life-preservers made
into a man—The Oyster Champion—Peter (not Guinea
Peter)—His friend John of York—Will the Devil have
him?—A Prince takes a Drink—The Pretty little Jew—
A Trio of True-men—O. P. F.—A Pair of F. F. V.'s, and
others of the like—The Magic Glass—Old Abe—A Quorum
arrive, and the Third Degree hold Session.

GET on your all-fours, gentle reader,
    And to yon darksome cavern creep;
And at the key-hole, gentle reader,
    Put on your spectacles, and peep!
Unskin the eye, and pick the ear,
And you shall see, and you shall hear.

Crawl, with our Chief and his good servant,
    Who go with sign and passing word—
With chivalry and ardor fervent,
    To get into Degree the Third.
Peep! while before the cave they crawl;
Listen! and hear and treasure all!

The Golden Circle brotherhood
Were quite a clever multitude;
        (36)

But this degree, as I suspect,
Was limited and quite select;
Its members not exceeding twenty—
And, for their purpose, 'twas a plenty.
They met to issue their decrees
To other, more enlarged degrees,
Keeping their purposes profound
Secreted darkly underground.

When Whillikens and his man Pete
Approached the third degree retreat,
The worthies of the secret forum
Were far too few to form a quorum.
Peep! by yon lantern burning blue,
You see none present yet but two—
Two—met betimes for woe or weal,
A secret wheel within a wheel.
There sit, upon a common level,
None but Jeff Davis and the Devil;
The one black-coated, stiffly starched,
The other hairy, somewhat parched:
The one lean, gaunt, and dignified,   .
The other bland and fiery eyed.
" My dearest Jeff," the devil said,
" Since you and I are firmly wed,
And pledged to work for one another,
I'll stick up to you like a brother.
But, if your looks do not belie us,
I really fear you're getting pious."(?)

" Good devil," little Jeff replied,
" My soul and body, hair and hide
Are all your own.   What shall I do
To prove my faithfulness to you ?"
The devil scraped his cloven foot,
And coughed, and spat a quart of soot,
And said, " My dear, so far, 'tis true,
I've had a willing slave in you;
You drink the potions that I mix;
You never shrink from dirty tricks;

You justify repudiation
With sanctified dissimulation ;
But can you render any reason
Why you have not committed treason ?"
   "Oh Lucifer ! I am surprised
To be so closely catechised.
In 1850 did I not
Assist in the disunion plot,
And fight in senate, night and day,
Against the compromise and Clay ?
Did I not run for governor,
And play disunion orator,
Till Mississippi, with her *Foote*,
Kicked Quitman and myself to-boot ?"

"Ah ! this, sly Jeff, is all a fact,
But *treason wants the overt act.*"

"Hold !" cried the little agitator,
"You know *the law would hang a traitor !*
If I *commit the crime in spirit,*
And slip the law, the more's the merit.
To do your will I will not falter,
But I confess I fear the halter.
Death by the rope ! I should despond !—
'Tis not so written in the bond.
Besides, if I was not outwitted,
Our contract should have benefitted
Your humble servant, even me,
As well as your high majesty."

"True, true, my spunky corporal,
The contract was reciprocal,
And I'll perform my stipulations
Up to your highest expectations.
'Tis eighteen hundred fifty-nine :
Ten years ago we both did sign
A solemn league and covenant
From which you never can recant.
You swore to set this glorious land

On fire, as with a blazing brand;
To get up a conspiracy,
And run mid-line from sea to sea,
This great Republic to dissever;
And then to be my slave forever:
I swore to make you president
Of half the country; and I meant
To have two nations side by side,
Where they in peace could not abide;
Where they should have unceasing 'spats,'
And fight, like the Kilkenny cats,
Till nothing but a little hair
Should show that either had been there.
    But I have now a better plot—
You'll join me in it, will you not?
Jeff, you are selfish, cold and callous,
And, if I'll save you from the gallows,
And show you how to play the traitor
So as to make your greatness greater
Would you object, my pretty boy,
The whole Republic to destroy?
Would you object to undermine
Fair Freedom's blood-cemented shrine,
And *on its ruins build a throne*,
If you could have it all your own?"

    The devil, as he threw the bait,
Drew up his hairy form in state;
Held his old pitchfork in his hand,
(His royal sceptre of command,)
And, with a chuckle, flashed his eye,
As Davis quickly made reply,
"Dear devil, if you'll save my throat,
I'll do it—damn me if I don't!"
    [Thought Pete, through key-hole peeping through,
    "He's sure to damn you if you do."]
Jeff, after but a second's pause,
Said, "How shall I escape the laws?"
    There was a quizzical, sly leer
In the red eye of Lucifer,

As thus he briefly made reply
In three small words, " *Bribe, steal, and lie !*"

The Colonel waited for awhile ;
But Old Nick held his breath to smile ;
And when Jeff found the devil dumb,
He urged him on : " Come, devil, come—
Speak freely now ; I am your man ;
Develop your infernal plan."
    " Give us your hand," replied Old Harry,
I swear the plot shall not miscarry.
I argued as a special pleader,
When, as Original Seceder,
I aimed, in the angelic schism,
At universal despotism.
Now Jeffie, by that knowing squint,
I see that you can take a hint."

" I see," cried little Jeff, " I see—
Secession is the talk for me,
And the fool populace, dod-rot 'em !
Shall know not what I've got at bottom.
I'll get up beautiful debates
Upon the rights of sov'reign states ;
Pretending to fulfill, you see,
John C. Calhoun's old prophecy.
'Twas eight and twenty years ago,
As near as I can guess, you know,
When the prophetic Nullifier,
.After he'd failed to work his wire ;
After old Hickory had ' coerced' him ;
After republicans had cursed him,
Said, like a wise philosopher,
' Car'lina is mine oyster :
She'll leave the Union at the hour
When free-state votes shall have the power
To govern by majority :
(A democrat I claim to be !
Now, if we work our cards aright,
When she goes out, sirs, just for spite,

The other slave-states, altogether,
Like sheep behind some big bell-wether,
Will jump the fence and follow after.'
Resuming, when he could for laughter,
'We'll have to back out now, my men,
To bide our time and hit again ;
We'll have to get the South united,
Pretending to have wrong things righted;
We'll have to lay a deeper plot,
And strike—not till the iron's hot.'
Thus far the statesman-sage could see
Into the dark futurity.
The iron heats ; the time draws nigh
When we shall make the cinders fly !
Our First Degree has done its part
In " firing up the Southern heart,"
And shall continue to create
Against free states relentless hate.
We'll warm them up to dissolution
By whining o'er the constitution ;
By preaching Southern rights, and trying
To agitate them by hard lying ;
And thus this popular degree
Shall blindly work for you and me.
    The second wheel in our machine,
Thinking the South is growing lean,
And wanting more of public platter
To make themselves a little fatter ;
And having failed in blustering
And Southern fillibustering,
Shall, with a little soft seduction,
Be made to talk of "reconstruction ;"
To talk of quitting old foundations
To build anew on slave relations ;
To tear down Freedom's homely shrine
That they may get up something fine ;
To balance scales with South and North,
And find out what the slaves are worth ;
To make four millions quite a plenty
Of weighing matter against twenty.

Besides, the second wheel, yon see,
Swear to obey the Third Degree.
The Third suppose the Southern States
Are to become confederates,
Conspire, and peacefully secede,
And form a nation great indeed ;
Where aristocracy shall batten
Upon the poor man's bones, and fatten ;
Where open, African 'free-trade'
Shall bring more negroes to their aid ;
Where ev'ry mush-head will be sure
To play official sinecure ;
In fine, where they shall live at ease,
And rule the country as they please.
  Now, my dear Nick, if we'll be smart,
These tools shall play a useful part,
And help us to despotic sway
Before they learn to rue the day."
Jeff, smiling, closed ; pulled up his collar,
And looked as beaming as a dollar.

The devil said, " The third wheel crew
Will do all that I tell them to ;
But you must not let ev'ry ass
Know that you're crawling in the grass
To wind yourself around the shrine
Where Freedom's burning censers shine,
To crush the hallowed altar stone,
And on its ruins build a throne—
No ! for I've had most willing tools
Who proved the very biggest fools.
Mind, ' Mum's the word :' unskin your eye ;
The motto is ' *Bribe, steal, and lie.*'"

"'Tis good advice," said Colonel Jeff;
I must play dummy, blind and deaf,
Wrap up in buckram dignity,
And let your minions work for me.
Of course I'll bribe, and steal, and lie,
But I will do it on the sly."

"Exactly so," replied Old Nick ;
"I always thought you up to trick,"
And with a loving sort of whack
He patted Davis on the back,
And said, "My precious little pet,
You have not all the lesson yet ;
You must not move till you are told
Who can be bought—who can be sold,
For if you cross one honest breast
You'll get into a hornet's nest."

"Dear Nick," said Jeff, "I have 'a fancy
That I may safely talk to Yancey,
A long tongued gent of honied word,
A penitentiary bird."

"Yes, there could surely be no balking
With him, and he *is* good at talking.
He has a strange presentiment
The South will make him president.
Your own self-interest, you know,
Will teach you, Jeff, how far to go.
He'll prove most excellent at play—
Should fighting come, he'll run away."

The fighting notion Jeff derided ;
"The North," he said, "are so divided,
So much afraid of being hissed
.And scorned as 'abolitionist,'
That they can't possibly combine
To cross the Mason-Dixon line."

The devil, with satanic guile,
Bowed down his head to hide a smile ;
Then, rising up, with smile suppressed,
Said, "Have you further to suggest ?"

"Perhaps," said Jeff, "that peaceful fellow,
Who fights no '*murderous*' duello ;
That sleek goose-feather-fighting Pryor,
Might serve me, as I want a liar."

"Poor stuff," the devil said, "but willing:
He'll run your errands for a shilling.
Just yoke him with his cousin Kitty;
And, in some ' Vigilance Committee,'
Or in some other mobbish clan,
Perhaps they both may make a man.
In this capacity receive them;
But as to lying, who'd believe them?"

"Perhaps, kind devil, if you please,
There's one among the F. F. V.'s,
A gray old hero, marked by scars
Of *shells*—received in *Oyster Wars*—
In whom our cause shall find a prize."

"Och!" cried the fiend, "you mean Old Wise?
Take him, but regulate his breath,
Or he will talk the cause to death.
I've no man—landshark or seafaring—
Who beats the governor at swearing.
I've none upon the 'sacred soil'
More closely fastened in my coil;
But he is such a cackling goose
I'm tempted oft to let him loose.
But as you want good agitators,
Set down his name among the traitors."

"I rather think I may depend
Upon brave Peter of Ostend:
In 1850 he was found
On revolutionary ground."

Replied his sooty majesty,
"Take my advice and let him be.
My very power he would retrench;
For he is so extremely French!
He's good at mouthing and grimaces,
But he will never work in traces;
He has ambition vaulting tall,
But in the grass he will not crawl;

He is sagacious, it is true,
But rather honest, Jeff, for you;
And if you should attempt to buy him,
He'll knock you down. Now, will you try him?
Why tremble so? And why such pallor?
You have the better part of valor.
Don't try old Peter: try his friend,
Old John of York, whose virtues blend
So happily, that out of h—l,
I love none better than Slidell."

Jeff Davis scanned the commentator—
He feared the fiend was playing traitor.
" How's this?" he cried; "You know old John
Would steal the ground he treads upon;
Would gamble only for himself,
And sell us all to pocket pelf.
I hate the man who disbelieves
The adage, ' Honor among thieves;'
I fear, if truth must be confessed,
To hug an adder to my breast.
You're shrewd—but I've a little wit,
And will not take your counterfeit.
If you don't want him down below,
'Tis very clear where he must go:
Just lead the saint of Plaquemine
Blindfolded through to Fiddler's Green."

" Hold!" yelled the fiend, in fire and smoke,
" I don't deserve the feeble stroke:
Why should you harbor such suspicion
When you and I are on one mission?
I am a foe to liberty
As staunch as you can ever be,
And I shall never mar our plan
By trusting an improper man.
I know Earl Houma's worth the trying--
And plotting, stealing, sneaking, lying,
Are just the qualities we néed,
If sovereign commonwealths secede

I pledge you, Jeffie, honor bright,
To make the gambler play aright ;
I promise too, you selfish sinner,
That none but you shall be the winner."
And milder grown, the princely plotter
Drank Jeffie's health in strong fire-water.

"I see you're right, we'll use the man,"
Replied the Mississippian ;
" His Janus face shall not delude us.
O, he will bring his little Judas,
So shrewd, so eloquent, so clever,
Who shuns gold never, *never, never !*
Both man and master, I may mention,
Have favor'd ' area extension'
While working for us in the second
Or India-rubber wheel.   I've reckoned
Upon the truckling of the Jew :
Bëelzebub, how will it do ?"

" 'Tis well," the devil answered briefly,
" But whom shall we depend on chiefly ?
What do you think of Floyd and Toombs,
And Cobb, and similar mushrooms ?"

" Ah ! Lucifer, I fear to say.
Perhaps they'd sell themselves for pay—
Perhaps they would—perhaps they wouldn't
I'd use them—I'm afraid I couldn't—
I know them well—you know them better—
Say, would they wear a golden fetter ? "

The old Arch Traitor laughed outright
To see poor Jeff in such a plight ;
For, with his cold, white-livered eyes,
And hollow cheeks, and whining cries,
And cautious speech, so half and half,
He did make e'n the devil laugh.

" Jeff, you are fool as well knave,"
Responded Nicholas, more grave.

" I've not on earth more servile grooms
Than those three pimps, Cobb, Floyd, and Toombs.
If you want hatred, blasphemy,
Bob Toombs will suit you to a T;
If you want mind of soul bereft;
If you want perjury and theft ;
If you want one to break an oath,
Or rob an armory, or both ;
If you want one of selfish lust,
Fit to betray official trust—
Fit to commit a matricide
On mother country, get supplied
In all these wants, with other spoil,
By calling on the 'sacred soil,'
In twilight shade or morning fog,
Upon John Floyd, the devil's dog.
   If you have any dirtier job,
Of course you'll have to call on Cobb "

Jeff rubbed his hands for very joy,
" And have you any more Old Boy ?"

" None quite so good.   But there is Buck
Who'd plod in dirt for party luck,
If party luck and party fodder
Would, in return, reward the plodder.
And there's another—Mr. Mason,
Who rings the slav'ry diapason ;
Who, to have liberty destroyed,
Will work almost as well as Floyd.
There's the Masonic brother Hunter,
Who moves 'accordingly to Gunter ;'
Once playing patriot *ex parte*,
Now playing partisan as smartly,
And growing better, till in season,
He'll like the very smell of treason.
And, should you need a hypocrite,
In Stephens you can make a hit :
He'd sell his creed, and bones, and vitals,
Soul, body, all—for empty titles.

Others there are, you'll know in time—
A criminal for every crime,
Soon here to meet in Third Degree,
Working, blindfold, for you and me,
While they suppose they play the traitor
To make themselves a little greater."

The stiff-necked czar-in-embryo,
His confidence in Nick to show,
Patted his patron on the head,
Caressed his horns, and coolly said,
"Just put me through, soon as you choose;
If I do win you cannot lose."

Now spoke his brimstone majesty
With a strong smack of prophecy :
"How soon these things shall come to pass
Is plainly figured in my glass.
I see 'Old Public Functionary'
With many a hopeful secretary,
With many a caucus congressman,
The presidential partisan.
Ha ! there is Floyd ! and Cobb ! and Black !
And there is the Thompsonian quack !
There are a dozen senators
All presidential counselors.
Mark yon sly figure in disguise,
Watching the gamblers with quick eyes,
And 'playing 'possum' to their faces,
While in his hand he holds the aces.
Jeff, see the image ere 'tis gone—
It is your own sweet *eidelon.*

Behold, while Black, with all his might,
Is proving O. P. F. all right ;
While Wigfall preaches constitution
And Yancey raises revolution,
Our Floyd is robbing for the South,
His sweet oath melting in his mouth ;
Our Cobb is stealing all the money,
And sucking perjury as honey ;

Our Mason talks of 'niggers' trying
To beat the little Jew at lying;
And our beloved Old Public Func,
Is either 'up to snuff' or drunk.
 Aha! see upstart soldiers prowling,
O'er mints and forts defenceless howling;
Army officers resigning,
The republic undermining;
Governors of states seceding,
Patriotic bosoms bleeding,
You and I together crowing
Over secrets worth the knowing,
While sits Old Public Func in stew,
Not knowing hardly what to do."

Here the devil stopped to chuckle
And fasten up his hair-bag buckle,
When he had taken out a few
Tobacco plugs for him to chew.
"Go on, talk on and chew your quid,"
Quoth Jeff; and so the devil did:
"Behold, within my magic glass,
Other personages pass;
There is a new chief magistrate——"
"Who? who?" cried Jeff, "I cannot wait,
I hope it is that dupe of ours——"
 "No, no! by the infernal powers,
It is old Abe!"

                Jeff bit his lips
And stood with hands upon his hips;
Then seized the glass, and further saw
Tall men who loved and feared the law,
Strong men whose arms were lifted high,
Who ready seemed to do or die;
Broad banners floating in the air,
And all the stars and stripes were there!
'Mid clouds of dust, the earth seemed quaking—
'Twas twenty-three white millions waking!
 4

'Mid storms, he saw the lightning glancing—
'Twas men of steel with steel advancing !
'Mid smoke and flame, the earth seemed dying
'Twas *the republic's purifying!*
'Mid gloom, light broke on freedom's sod—
'Twas the triumphant smile of God !

Jeff saw another vision pass—
A hanging scene ! he dropped the glass,
Fell to the ground in deep despair.
" Traitor !" he cried, " you've played unfair !"
He cursed his patron to his face,
And wished him to a hotter place.

The devil is a story teller,
And what some call a " right smart feller ;"
So he said nothing for a while,
But wore a consequential smile ;
And then, in quite a winning way,
Spat out tobacco juice to say,
" You've used my magic glass, my friend
By looking through the little end ;
You turned the instrument about
And saw all things reversed, no doubt.
Cheer up ! cheer up ! my gallant pet,
You'll be a live dictator yet ;
With our ' peculiar institution,'
We'll work a *peaceful revolution ;*
With motto, ' bribe and steal and lie,'
We'll triumph, Jeffie, you and I."
And with his stiff forefinger, he
Tickled Jeff's ribs prodigiously.

" I'm satisfied, since you have spoken,
But sorry that the glass is broken ;
And since I have beheld, my friend,
Secession from the other end,
And since I can't have further view,
Pray tell me, devil, is it true
That old Abe will be president ?"

" Yes, such is my presentiment—
You saw the old rail-splitting hound
Before the glass was turned around."

"Then surely we shall have to buy him."

"No !" said the fiend, "no use to try him ;
Old Abe is honest, and I hate him—
Fortune nor fame can ever bait him ;
Old Abe is able, I can't rule him,
Nor can designing men befool him.
The only thing for him I swagger,
Is the assassin's midnight dagger !"

"That's capital ! you know the fable
Of holy writ, that *Cain* killed Abel ;
Old Abe is *able*, you have stated :
We'll have the fable illustrated !"
With this Jeff laughed a cold, dry laugh,
The devil bellowed like a calf.
Scared by the bellow, Guinea Pete
Jumped from the keyhole to his feet,
And then fell back upon the trunk
Of Whillikens, asleep and drunk ;
And this waked Whillikens, who swore
Louder than he did snore before ;
And this broke up the dialogue
Between the devil and his dog.
The former sank, with rumbling sound,
Down deeper—deeper underground ;
The latter turned the cavern key
To open for the Third Degree.
    Pleased to believe a drunken ear
Had been the only listener,
And that all the alarming rattle
Had been made only by a chattel,
He sat him down within the door,
And ne'er had looked so meek before.
Said Peter, "Masser, I dare say
You'se been in dat ar cave to pray !"

The Golden Circle brotherhood
    Came, one by one, and formed a quorum,
When they before the door had stood
And shown by signs that they were good
    And worthy to compose the forum.

More than a dozen—less than two—
    Sat where had lately sat the devil ;
Men whose names are known to you,
Men whose claims were shown to you
    When Nick and Jeff sat on a level.

What was thought and what was said ;
    What was done and what was plotted,
Need not agitate your head :
They were by Jeff Davis led,
    By Bëelzebub besotted.

And they swore to lie and cheat,
    Steal and murder !   Noble braves
Put their necks 'neath Jeffie's feet
So willingly that Guinea Pete
    Said "Niggers aint de only slaves."

They swore to turn the outer wheels
    By many a plausible pretence ;
To make them run around like reels—
Blind fools ! their working was the deil's
    From centre to circumference !

BOOK V.

THE REBEL.

Sir Knight a little Groggy—He is the Chief of the Seceders
—Cockade and Cocktail—Rattlesnake—Buck's Cabinet—
Devil Tracks—G. Whillikens' Coat-tail badly pulled—
"Submissionists"—Sir Knight takes Mints and Mint-
Juleps—Takes Fortified Vacuums—Jeff tickles him—G.
Whillikens, K. G. C., has his Dulcinea—Guinea Pete's
Philosophy of the Impending War—Seceders rushing the
States out—Delegates to State Conventions assuming the
power of electing Delegates to Montgomery—They have
the good taste to elect themselves—Turn out to be a
Congress—They elect Jeff and get Stephens out of the
way—Peaceful Fillibustering—Jeff lies a little—The
Forts which Sir Knight had not taken—Little "Beauty"
—8000 gain a Victory over 70 Men—Beauregard and the
Jews—Jeff addresses the Devil and makes a Slight Mis-
take—A Serenade.

" I'LL split old Uncle Sam in two !
 I'll bust the Union like a punkin !
1st, 'Cause I've nothing else to do ;
 2nd, Because a little drunken.
Come, Peter, join the cho-ri-ous
Of glorious ! and glorious ! !"
So sang G. Whillikens, with toddy
Bubbling within his bloated body,
As from the meeting he did go
The Southern generalissimo.
 Beside bell-buttons and long blade,
And all that our First Book displayed,
He sported now a blue cockade—
Cockade without, cocktail within,—
This held by stomach, that by pin.

Besides, he added to his charms
The new secession coat of arms,
And bore his banner o'er the soil,
Stamped with the rattlesnake in coil.
Our knight, with sword of battle drawn,
Went singing as he wabbled on,
" I'll split old Uncle Sam in two !
    I'll make two nations without trouble :
1st, 'Cause I am a little blue ;
    2nd, Because I can see double.
Come, Peter, join the cho-ri-ous
Of glorious ! and glorious ! !"

Our knight went singing, wabbling on
Until he got to Washington,
Where president and cabinet
Patted his back and called him " pet ;"
Where warmest friends of O. P. F.
Were sitting cheek-by-jowl with Jeff ;
Where grave, official double-dealers—
Indian-bond and money stealers—
Powder, ball, and cannon robbers
Were the presidential jobbers.
" G. Whillikens looks fat and hearty ;—
I hope his cause will help *the party*,"
Said O. P. F., "but if there's doubt,
Just hold on till my time is out ;
I could behold my country die,
But not *the party*—let me fly."
Said Jeff unto our champion,
" All things are right in Washington."
To Pete the truth was very bare,
The devil had been lately there.
Pleased with Cobb-stolen public purse,
Our knight sang out another verse :
" I'll split old Uncle Sam in two !
    I'll rend the ship of state asunder :
1st, 'Cause I want to put him through ;
    2nd, Because I want the plunder.
Come, Peter, join the cho-ri-ous
Of glorious, glo-o-rious !"

Forth from the capital G. Whill-
Ikens did go his fame to fill,
With high officials in his trail
All holding to his bob coat-tail.
He traveled through the sovereign states ;
And sovereign governoŕs, with baits
Of sweetest treason did invite :
He did not fail to "get a bite ;"
And, with his man-hooks in their jaws,
He drew them on in glory's cause.

Some sovereign people seemed to be
At first opposed to tyranny :
G. Whillikens, with doubled fists,
Denounced them as "Submissionists,"
And they from their positions came
Like rats from barn-house in a flame. .
They'd been prepared for this, you see,
By labors of the First Degree,
And now were driven by.a word
To give up blindly to the Third.

Now from the fields, the dales, the dells,
The party clubs, the gambling hells,
The gutters and slave-dealers' pens,
Came the loud cry, " G. Whillikens !"

Our fat man did not listen long
Till he responded in a song :
" I'll split old Uncle Sam in two !
    I'll make the eagle shed his feathers !
1st, 'Cause 'twill please Jeff D. & Co.
    2nd, Because I've nigger fellers.
Come, Peter, join the cho-ri-ous
Of glorious ! and glorious !"

The chivalry at once enlisted,
Thinking ne'er to be resisted ;
Boasting that one gentleman
Could whip six of the Northern clan,

Should any Northern clan presume
To save the country from its doom.
G. Whillikens, now just for sport,
Took many an armory and fort—
Supplied with arms which Mr. Floyd
Had sent to have the land destroyed.
G. Whillikens did also take,
(Marching beneath the rattle-snake,)
Custom-houses, mints and money,
Just because he felt so funny—
Felt the teeming of the toddy,
And could frighten any body.

" Go it !" cried the lean Dictator,
" You're half horse, half alligator ;
You're a fat old snapping turtle,
You're Knight of the Golden Circle.
Hail, Southern Generalissimo !
Pity you have no stronger foe
Than Uncle Sam, for you can wipe
Him out with but a single swipe !"

For answer, fatty did no worse
Than sing to Jeff another verse :
" I'll split old Uncle Sam in two ;
    I'll run my broadsword through his body ;
1st, 'Cause 'twill please such folks as you ;
    2nd, Because I'm full of toddy.
Come, Peter, join the cho-ri-ous,
Of glory, glory, glorious !"
Said Jeff, " Sir Knight, fat man of sport,
Hero of many an empty fort,
You have a squire, (though rather shady,)
But knight should also have his lady
So that he could go forth to fight,
Pledged to his lady and the right.
I know some excellent old women,
With whom our cause would go on swimmin'—
There's Mrs. Jackson of Missouri,
Who would accept ye, I assure ye ;

And in Virginny, Widow Tyler,
Who would say 'yes,' or 'bust her biler.'
Go, G. Whillikens, and get ye
To yourself a precious Betsy."

"Jeff," said G. Whillikens, "my heart
Has had its lady from the start;
My first campaign, in Carolina,
I fought for glory and my Dinah:
She's the 'Peculiar Institution:'
And, 'till the Union's dissolution,
I'll battle for my 'ladye-love'
And blast the land to save my dove."

Said Jeff, "'Tis well.   Come, take a drink?
I like your nose—how very pink!
A little whiskey's good, you see,
To bolster up your chivalry."
Said Pete, "He'll hark him on, I hope—
Dat is de softest sort of soap."
Our knight his battles did rehearse,
And then sang Jeff another verse,
Something about his reigning o'er us,
And calling Pete to join the chorus.

This artful dodger, Guinea Pete,
Eavesdropper at the cave retreat,
Told not that at the secret grotto
Jeff had approved the devil's motto;
That he had even sold himself
To the old Cloven-foot for pelf;
But said, "Ole boss, you fight for Jeff;
I know you's brave, I smell yer bref;
Dat whiskey makes de gents enlist
To fight de 'abolitionist.'
De white folks are to pull de trigger,
But dis ar war can't hurt de nigger."
Pete did not say, but well he knew
Just what the devil meant to do;
And he concluded, (the sly knave,)
The slave could not be worse than slave;

And that while wheels were turning 'round
. The lower spokes might leave the ground;
And that, 'mid war's chaotic revel,
He might get free, spite of the devil.
"There'll be no war, you silly fool,
I'll just display this fighting tool,
And all the Union men, no doubt,
Will look at me and fizzle out.
I'll split old Uncle Sam in two;
    I'll tear the stars and stripes to tatters :
1st, 'Cause I've got up something new;
    2nd, Because Jeff Davis flatters.
Come, Peter, join the cho-ri-ous,
Of glorious! and glorious ! !"

So sung the Knight of th' Golden Circle,
And Jeffie crowned his brow with myrtle,
Saying, "We'll stand and work the wires,
And note whatever next transpires;
We may discover states seceding,
Without the slightest drop of bleeding,
If you will only show your nose,
And swear to kill all who oppose."

Now sundry sovereign governors
Called legislative counselors,
Who bade the subject-people meet
And place themselves beneath the feet
Of wise conventions, whether they
Desired to meet or stay away.
    These wise conventions, (not elected
If devil tricks were all detected,)
Passed sovereign edicts, there's no doubt,
By which they kicked the people *out*,
While they retained themselves *in* power,
And still stay in till this good hour;
Refusing yet to put to vote
Whether a state would cut her throat.
"Here," said the sauciest of blacks,
"I see de debbil's cloven tracks."

They next proceeded—harmless elves—
To choose the best among themselves,
To hold a Southern States Convention
Against the popular intention.
It surely would have been absurd
To counsel with the vulgar herd,
And take their votes for them to show
Whether the states should meet or no ;
And to elect the delegates,
Should they, by vote, convene the states.

These self-appointed state committees,
In one of Alabama's cities,
Had hardly time to take a seat,
When, metamorphosis complete !
As Halcyon changed to feathered songstress,
This body made themselves *a Congress!*

Now wasn't it strange ! to us, I mean—
Though doubtless plain behind the screen ;
For Guinea says he saw "for certain,
A hairy hand behind de curtain."

The Congress had a secret sitting :
The devil, (simple men outwitting,)
Put forward, for the *sovereign nations,*
Our country's chart, with emendations,
Because the sovereign of the air
Would play the farce of playing fair.
It was a humbug—well he knew it,
But folks near-sighted saw not through it ;
He meant thus fairly to begin,
That he might get the honest in,
Then give the chart an overhaul,
And put in slave-trade, snakes and all,
And finally to take a feather
And knock it over altogether.
This was his counterplot, I know :
Pete heard him tell Jeff Davis so.

The next step which *the Congress* went
Was to make Jeff the president—

Not chairman of the dyed committee,
For Cobb was that—(oh what a pity,
They had no more secreted place
Where the old thief could hide his face!)
But Jeff was made chief magistrate
Of states y'clept "confederate;"
Though not a citizen, I know,
E'er cast a vote to make him so.

"Congress" consulted once or twice,
Who should be nominated "vice:"
Then, just to stop his Union speeches,
Put Stephens in official breeches
Which could have done, without the wearer,
The duties of this office bearer.

"Congress" endorsed the Golden Knight
For taking forts without a fight;
For taking governmental mint
With cash and bullion that was in't,
And custom-houses, to be made
The Southern *depots* of free trade.
All this the Congress, wide awake,
Did from the sovereign captors *take*—
Did from the sovereign nations wring
By *peaceful fillibustering*;
And in their treasury entombed it,
Or, as Jeff Davis says, "assumed it."

G. Whillikens was overjoyed
To find he'd been so well employed
In robbing property, and swore
He would go on and capture more;
But, ere he started on the wing,
Halted for Jeff to hear him sing
Of cutting Uncle Sam in twain,
While Peter joined him in refrain.

As Jeff, (but late a soft soap slosher,)
Was now chief cook and bottle washer,

He stood upon his dignity;
And, venting his malignity
Against his kin in yankee land,
Said he had rather take a hand
In open field where life is spent,
Than be the Southern President;
That he ne'er cherished aspirations
To rule *confederated nations.*
   "Wonder," said Guinea, on the sly,
Whether a president can lie?"

"Jeff," said our hero, fat and greasy,
"You'd find the fighting mighty easy—
Easy as when your Bissell foe
You challenged—then backed out, you know;
Easy as when you showed white feather,
Lest you and Judas come together;
Easy, because 'tis only sport
To take full mint or empty fort;
Easy because the Southrons say
The yankees will all stay away;
Easy, because the gentlemen's
Commander is G. Whillikens!"

"Between ourselves, sir knight, you're right;
But we must make a show of fight.
Chief magistrate I'll stoop to be,
While you lead on the chivalry,
Of which you are the very flower;
I'll join you in the battle hour."
And Jeff might have gone on to say,
"I'll join at close of battle day."

As schoolboy, spoiling for a fight,
Putting himself in *milling* plight,
Cool as a cucumber or colder,
Stands with a chip upon his shoulder,
And dares each youngster pugilist
To knock it over with his fist,
So stood old Uncle Sam, arrayed
With chip on either shoulder blade,

With Sumter here and Pickens there.
Exclaiming, " Hit them, if you dare !"

Said Jeff, " Sir knight, what will you do ?"

" *I'll split old Uncle Sam in two*——"
Jeff couldn't stand this endless hammer,
He lost his temper and his grammar ;
" G. Whillikens, you and your nigger,
Stop your singin', drop the figger,
And tell me with no idle sports,
You'll undertake to take the forts ?"

The Golden Circle knight replied,
" I guess *them forts* have men inside !"
Said Jeff, " Fort Sumter sure must fall,
Manned with but seventy in all ;
You, with eight thousand Southern men,
Are sure to whip three score and ten."

" But seventy ?" cried Guinea's lord ;
" Eight thousand and my dangling sword
Can conquer seventy with ease,
And make the cowards knock their knees."

" 'Tis said they hav'n't much to eat—
So they cannot be hard to beat." ·

" The impudent, lean, hungry hounds,
To dare to stand on Southern grounds !
As Gray-eyed Man of Destiny,
As Fillibuster, K. G. C.,
I soon shall set Fort Sumter free—
Hip, hip, hurrah !"
                    The hero fat
Being rotund and rather squat,
Making a flourish, over tumbled,
And on the pavement rolled and rumbled
Until his body servant, Pete,
Put him again upon his feet.

G. Whillikens now blew his whistle,
To summon soldiery of gristle,
For Sumter's fight.
                    By blowing hard,
He called G. Toussant Beauregard;
The same who in the crescent city
Once raised a vigilance committee
To help himself to office gear—
At least five thousand by the year;
The same who robbed an arsenal
For purposes political,
And, when he'd thus committed treason
For a pecuniary reason,
Shot off his cannon down the street,
And, butcher-like, killed his own meat!
His living troops, to flee the slayer,
Ran off and left him—*not the* mayor

Beholding this, Old Public Func
Gave office to this man of spunk,
Although 'twas fully understood
He'd do more treason if he could;
Would quit the crib which fed him well,
And join the South should she rebel.

G. Beauregard, G. Whillikens,
G. Pete, eight thousand citizens—
In Charleston made a mighty splutter;
Eight thousand full of bread and butter—
Fat thousands fighting hungry tens,
Fat thousands and G. Whillikens!

Sir knight looked upward in the air—
The stars and stripes were floating there;
"My chivalry! my knighthood's pride!
Cut down that saucy rag," he cried.

Bang! went the balls, and *whizz!* the shells,
For many hours, as story tells;

It is a pity that we failed
To get the old rail-splitter nailed,
While passing on through Baltimore ;
Pity his abolition gore
Was sprinkled not upon the stand
Where he made oath to save the land !
O, dearest devil, how we hated
To see Old Abe inaugurated !

But I've no reason to complain :
Rebels come fast as drops of rain ;
Besides the 'Trumps of Third Degree,'
The lower 'lodges' swarm to me ;
I've many governors in action,
From Pickens down to Mrs. Jackson ;
So, if one traitor turns aside,
Or if one victim saves his hide,
Our glorious cause cannot miscarry,
While thus upheld by you, Old Harry."

Here Peter stooped to scratch his wool,
But spoke not, though his heart was full ;
Jeff took it as a compliment,
A bowing to *The President :*
He said the devil listened well,
And thus went on, his pride to swell :

" Already I'm *The President !*
To Washington my course is bent ;
Within the White-House, I'll reside
'Till fifteen states are on my side ;
Then I'll invade the free-states border
And there create so much disorder,
And get up such an anarchy
That for peace-sake, they'll come to me ;
And thus, 'till all the Union States
Join my hood-winked Confederates.
The war will surely be one-sided,
For the North is so divided
That old Lincoln never can
Get up an army.   Curse the man !

Thus, when I've all the people down,
I'll step from chaos to a crown,
And all the land shall wildly burst
And yell, 'Long live King Jeff, the First!' "

" Don't count de chickens, 'fore der hatch d,"
Laughed Guinea Pete, as he unlatched
The stable door, and bolted out.
Then said, when out of reach, no doubt,
" King Jeff, you cut a purty figger
Standin' an' talkin' with a nigger !"

Jeff placed himself on no such level,
He meant to hob-nob with the devil
And not to talk an hour you see
Unto a piece of property.
Of course he felt somewhat disgusted :
But soon his temper was adjusted,
For Whillikens with his cockade,
Regaled him with this serenade :
" I'll split old Uncle Sam in two :
    I'll tread upon him when he's dying;
1st, Cause he must give place to you,
    2nd, Because I'm fond of lying.
" Come Peter, join the cho-ri-ous !
Come Beaury, sing victorious !
Come Jeffie and reign over us,
Glory, glory, glorious !"

And forty verses more he sung
'Till Jeffie from the stable sprung,
And donkeys raised so loud a bray
It scared the Muses all away.

BOOK VI.

THE GREAT-USED-UP.

Old Abe—He hears News—Writes a little Note—The. People
answer it—Jeff astonished and hurt—He has a Talk with
G. Whillikens—Sir Knight is ready for a Big Fight—.
Little Beaury & Co., U. S. A.—Battle begun—Bishop
Polk—The North "Compromising"—Magruder's Whiskey
—Pillow's Yankee Notions—The Hero of Oysters—Mrs.
Jackson preserving her character—Guinea Pete with his
Zouaves D'Afrique—The Knight of the Golden Circle a
little scared—Old Twiggs rather suspicious—Texas Cow-
drivers—Red Indians—G. Whillikens in a stew—White
feathers—The Contrabands—Feelings, Sayings, and Do-
ings—President Davis rides up—The Smoke of Battle
clears away—Star-light—The last glimpse of the Golden
Circle—G. Whillikens melts away and is seen no more.

OLD Abe sat in the corner winking ;
Owl-like, said nothing but kept thinking ;
Lamb-like, was silent under curses;
Job-like, was patient 'mid reverses,
Till from the South the message came
That Sumter fort was in a flame ;
That rebel guns had fired upon
The great free-land of Washington,
And that the flag our mothers wrought—
The flag for which our fathers fought—
The flag which they bequeathed in trust,
Had been down-trodden in the dust !
Then Abe stood up and coolly wrote
The people quite a simple note—
'Twas on a little piece of paper :
Who would have thought so small a taper
Could set the country in a blaze,
And boil the blood of other days ?

(68)

Ah ! there was fluid in the scroll
Which could electrify the soul,
And thrust a burning, lightning thrill
Through yeomanry of iron will !
　　Yes, there was something written there,
Which, read aloud in open air,
Brought back ten thousand echoings
From Bunker Hill and Eutaw Springs ;
From Princeton, Yorktown, Brandywine ;
From Vernon's Mount, the Pilgrim's Shrine ;
From Thames, Chalmette, and Lundy's Lane ;
From battle scenes on ocean main ;
From Mexico where heroes bled ;
From sepulchres of martyred dead—
The echoes came upon the ear
In thunder peals—the deaf might hear—
" Our flag is trodden in the dust :
Be faithful to your mighty trust !"

Feeling their very heart-strings thrill,
The people cried " We will !　We will ! !"
The great awakening of all
When Freedom's Chief had made the call ;
And when our honored, martyred braves
Had called again from bloody graves,
Seemed like the rising from the sod
When all shall hear the trump of God !

Responsive to the strong appeal,
Five hundred thousand men of steel
Sprung full-armed from their country's breast,
And marched to rescue the oppressed—
To fight the battles of the free—
To save their father's legacy—
To bear aloft Columbia's star
To quell the *matricidal war !*

Poor Jeff ! alas ! what could he do ?
He found himself in quite a stew !

He saw the Union men arising,
And said he thought it most surprising;
He ne'er had dreamed they had the spunk:
They must be crazy now, or drunk—
Mad as March hares to make assault
On him—a man without a fault!
On him—the saint-like, peaceful one,
Whose wish was to be let alone!
On his meek followers, who say
For quiet homes they ever pray!

G. Whillikens! He gave a snort,
Ordered his grog and drank a quart,
And swore to whip his yankee cousins—
Each Southern man could kill his dozens.

Said Jeff, "Sir knight, we didn't begin it;
We're in the game, and we must win it,
For *necks* as well as hearts are in it."
Said Whillikens, "I'll take a drink—
I'll give the chivalry the wink,
And the old Ship of State must sink."
Said Jeff, "The rattlesnake is eyeing—
Charming the eagle bird, or trying;
Thus will I charm the North, by lying."
Said Whillikens, "The snake shall rattle—
Switching his tail before the battle:
Thus I'd approach the Union cattle."
Said Jeff, "To guard against disaster,
You must enlist the soldiers faster:
The slave should battle for his master."
Said Whillikens, "Suppress your fears:
I gather up my *volunteers*
By sticking guns behind their ears;
And the most chicken-hearted choose
To put their necks within my noose—
Off go their heads if they refuse!
The slaves shall be entrenchment diggers,
But rest in fight, to pull gun-triggers;
Half of the Southern strength is niggers."

Said Gu:nea, speaking with great meekness,
" Dat sort of strength may prove yer weakness !"
Helter-skelter, rumpsy-dumpsy,
Went our civilized Tecumseh,
O'er the mighty land of cotton
Till quite ready he had gotten—
And just then, when he'd begun
To take up march to Washington,
His big eyes saw that in his way
The "Northern hordes of Lincoln" lay,
And, in his highway to the West,
He saw another hornet's nest ;
And on the road between the two,
More "hireling troops" were in review.
He swore it was a Yankee trick
To get an army up so quick.

G. Whillikens was more excited
Than he had been since he was knighted.
He reared, he pitched, he snorted loud
Amid his military crowd ;
He spouted like a mighty whale
About to switch its awful tail !
" Soldiers !" he cried, " these coward cattle
Invade your soil to give you battle—
Rush to the thickest of the fight !
Strike for Jeff Davis and the right !"
Then turning to their officers,
He thundered in their open ears,
" Ho ! Johnston, Lee, and Beauregard,
    Deserters from the U. S. A.,
Lead on—' our homes,' the fighting word ¡
    The devil is to pay.
Drive from Virginia's ' sacred soil'
Virginians who would despoil
    Our castles—in the air :
Drive them—or 'twill be very much
Like Holland taken by the Dutch,
    And we shall be—nowhere !

The soldier's honor bids you be
True to your treachery !"
Each faithful brigadier addressed,
Slapped his right hand upon his breast,
Then waved on high his battle-blade,
And onward led his brave brigade.
There flowed the Union flag of stars—
Here the secession blots and bars—
    The battle was begun !
It was a rain of shot and shell—
A fire as if the mouth of hell
    Had opened to the sun !
From ocean to the western waste,
The line of battle could be traced—
    A line of livid flame !
The cannon thundered peal on peal ;
There was the sound of clashing steel,
    And sounds—too sad to name !

" Ho ! Most Right Reverend General,
    Bold hero of the bushy robe,
Go, revel in Death's carnival,
    Be bloodiest bishop of the globe !
Strike for the stretch of slavery,
Strike for your university,
Strike for secession anarchy,
    And for G. Whillikens !"
The bishop raised his pious eye
And made a suitable reply,
    And closed with two Amens !

The thundering artillery,
Roaring—roaring dreadfully,
    Was heard from shore to shore—
The Union's answer to the South ;
The compromise at cannon's mouth,
    " The country—evermore !"
But still the Golden Circle knight,
Swore Unionists could never fight,

(For he was growing light and frisky
On Magruder's rotten whiskey ;)
And he cried to old Magruder,
" Drive the insolent intruder
Backward, with his hireling slaves,
Or welcome them to bloody graves !
The chivalry must find it play
To whip the yankees any day."
" Hurrah ! hurrah !" the soldiers shouted,
" Every coward shall be routed !"

While yet the knightly chieftain spoke,
There rose a denser, blacker smoke,
As if the day were turned to night,
With lightning flash, the only light—
Could cowards stand in such a fight ?

"Oh Gideon, the wondrous ditcher ;
Oh, Gideon, the river hitcher,
    What are you planning there ?
The driftwood, coming after rain,
Broke up *your Mississippi chain*,
    Now, do you fix a snare ?
O, quit your head-work, Gideon,
March on ! the battle shall be won,
    The foe is but a hare !"
Said Gideon, " If I must, I must ;
But I'm afraid my guns will bu'st
    And throw me in the air !"

Now Gideon got up his steam,
And with his fleet he got up stream ;
But finding he had made a blunder,
Steamed down again to 'scape big thunder,
And looked like dog with tail stuck under.

Our hero, riding on his mare,
Was here, and there, and everywhere ;
He snorted like a frightened colt,
And swore he was a thunderbolt,

And cried out, "Where's old Wise,
   Hero of oysters?   Strike the blow,
The Unionists to ostracise—
   Your vengeance on the foe!
Go—rush into the scene of action—
Alas! there goes poor Mrs. Jackson!
She flies, as 'tis her woman duty,
Before the banner, 'Booty-Beauty;'
She flies in haste to save her honor,
With all her skirts and hoops upon her!"

Still stood the Union legions true
To their beloved Red, White and Blue;
Denounced as most fanatical,
They seemed sedately practical,
E'en while the heavens above were red,
And earth below was strewn with dead.

G. Whillikens, a little "tight,"
Now said the yankee fools might fight,
And that a patriotic clown,
Might chance to get his "betters" down;
But trying to suppress his tremor,
He cried "Huzza!" and waved his streamer,
"Never, never beat retreat—
Lead on the niggers, Guinea Pete!"
The darkies answered Guinea's horn,
"We're comin', jest as shore's yer born!"
The sable legion, *Zouave D'Afrique,*
Soldiers bought and sold in traffic,
Were brought to battle by their masters,
To save their "quarters" from disasters.
"Pete," cried Sir Knight, "lead on to glory!
We've got into a category——"
"*Cat*—what?"
               "None of your saucy lip!
I mean they've got us on the hip;
Go, native Southrons, and resist
The savage abolitionist;

Go, slaves, and lay the tyrant low,
Repel the freedom-loving foe ;
Go and reduce the North to ashes,
Or each shall have a hundred lashes.
Now, mind you, Pete, none of your jaw."
The negroes answered, " Yah ! yah ! yah !"
And marched into the cloudy smoke,
Where loud was heard the battle stroke.

Still heroes fought and heroes fell—
   There was a crimson flood,
As if the open mouth of hell
   Were belching human blood !

G. Whillikens grew more excited,
Perhaps a little—bit—affrighted ;
'Twas evident the chivalry
Felt small—though each behind his tree ;
But Whillikens cried " Rally ! rally !
Make another bloody sally,
' Neck or nothing' is the word,
' Death by swinging or the sword !'
Halloo ! Old Twiggs ! You must remain
   Far in the rear ! Don't want you here—
You might desert your troops again—
   Stick to New Orleans and small beer !
M'Culloch, bring your cattle-drivers,
Lasso-ropers, bowie-knivers ;
On ! with demon resolution,
For the ' Sacred Institution !' "
Where the Indians ? Hark ! their yells,
Heard amid the bursting shells,
Tell the place where savage rage
Resists the progress of the age ;
Where Barbarism blindly wars
Against bold Freedom's Flag of Stars !
Ah ! vain the conflict ! Onward goes
The banner over savage foes—
They gnash their teeth in dying breath,
By their allies betrayed to death.

The Golden Knight looked in despair
As he went riding on his mare ;
His whiskey would not brace his nerves ;
He feared to call on Twiggs' reserves ;
He had no faith in Gideon's snares,
Nor any in the Bishop's prayers ;
Johnston, and Beauregard, and Lee,
Old mud-stick Wise, tactic Hardee,
Green, Price, and many such as they,
Had found the fighting more than play,
And, much unlike their boasted habits,
Were running like so many rabbits !
" They fly !   They fly !" in clarion tones
Was heard amid the dying groans.

Sir Knight half thought his army spoke
Amid the shroud of flame and smoke
And that the foe was in retreat
Before the hosts of Guinea Pete.
" Who fly ?   The Abolition hordes
Before the Sable Legion's swords ?"
The negroes answered " Yah ! yah ! yah !
De black must mind de white man's law—
    Now, massers, don't ye scold ;
Yer property is changing hand,
We niggers is all contraband ;
    O, massers, you is sold !"

G. Whillikens—what could he do ?
His visage turned red, white, and blue,
As if the country's stars and stripes
Were taking their daguerreotypes
Upon his face.   His portly belly
Trembled just like a piece of jelly !
The Hero of the Southern Nation
Was melting fast by perspiration !

Still rang the welkin with the shout
" They fly !   The foe is put to rout—"

" Who fly ?" cried Fatty, with a stutter.
Pete answered, smooth as bread and butter,
" De patriarchs is runnin' out
'*Cause dey've no slaves to fight about ;*
Ise gwine to take my Sable Legion
Off to de abolition region ;
Good bye, ole boss ! you and your cotton,
Shall never, never be forgotten."

G. Whillikens foamed at the mouth,
And swore the negroes of the South
Were traitors all, and ought to be
Just whipt to death for treachery.
Pete touched his nose and twirled his hand,
Exclaiming, " *We is contraband !*"
Pete merely answered, when berated,
" Dis property is confiscated !"

The Rebel Chieftain foamed and fretted,
Cursed and cried and swelled and sweated,
Till a fit of melancholy,
Made him mutter "golly !" "golly !"
Then he sat upon his mare,
The picture of sublime despair !
And finally, the people say,
He sweated, melted all away.

But who is he, so fresh and bold,
    Just coming at the close of battle ?
Alas ! poor Jeffie, you are sold !
" They fly !" but not as you were told !
You cannot get the reins to hold ;
Nor as the victor be extolled—
    You didn't win the battle !
You cannot have your crown of gold—
    Your throat begins to rattle !
Aha ! here comes your friend of old,
With cloven foot—Jeff, you're a-cold—
    He has a claim to settle !
Don't shiver, Jeffie, but behold

The friend with whom you once cajoled—
See him his coil of hemp unfold—
    You are a man of mettle—
Ife means to draw you through the mold,
    And boil you in his kettle !
*   *   *   *   *   *

The storm is past—the sky is fair—
And all the stars are shining there !
And by their new-lit beams I see
The Golden Circle, Third Degree,
Each member hanging on a tree !

THE END.